This book belongs to:

. . . .

. . . .

Timmy the cat

To Tricia, Mike,
   Yasmin and Natasha
              – with love

To find out more about
Simon James and his books visit
www.simonjamesbooks.com

First published 2002 by Walker Books Ltd
87 Vauxhall Walk, London SE11 5HJ

This edition published 2008

10 9 8 7 6 5 4 3 2 1

© 1989, 2002, 2008 Simon James

This book has been typeset in ITC Usherwood

Printed in China

British Library Cataloguing in Publication Data:
a catalogue record for this book is
available from the British Library

ISBN 978-1-4063-0847-1

www.walkerbooks.co.uk

SIMON JAMES

The Day Jake Vacuumed

WALKER BOOKS
AND SUBSIDIARIES

LONDON • BOSTON • SYDNEY • AUCKLAND

Jake was difficult.
Jake was a problem.
He didn't like doing
anything for anyone.

So you can imagine how Jake felt when one day his mother asked him to do the vacuum cleaning.

For a while, Jake played with the machine, enjoying the loud noise it made.

Then a really wicked idea occurred to him.
Very quietly he crept over to Timmy, the cat.
Aiming the nozzle at Timmy, Jake switched on
the vacuum cleaner and sucked up the poor cat!
Jake was delighted.

Jake knew he would be in trouble.
I might as well make it BIG TROUBLE! thought Jake.
He sneaked off to the kitchen …

and sucked his mother up into the
vacuum cleaner, rubber gloves and all!

"Yippee. I'm free!" shouted Jake.
"No one to tell me to do anything!"
He had the whole house to himself,
except, that is, for his sister upstairs.

Jake's sister was in her bedroom,
playing with her dolls.
In crept Jake.
He climbed on top of the cupboard
and switched on the vacuum cleaner.
You can imagine what happened then.

But, oh dear! Jake remembered
that his father would be home soon.
There was only one thing to do.

At six o'clock on the dot, Jake's father opened
the front door. Out jumped Jake with the
vacuum cleaner roaring on full power.
It was a difficult fit at first, but eventually …
POP! In went Jake's father.
"Hooray!" shouted Jake.

Jake was delighted.
At last he was in charge!
He was so pleased that he decided to
suck up the WHOLE room, and indeed,
the whole page of this book …

leaving only himself and the vacuum
cleaner. Jake was free.

But Jake hadn't noticed that the vacuum cleaner was now stuffed to bursting point and about to explode.

And explode it did, with a gigantic bang!
Once Jake's parents had recovered, they were furious.
They sent him to bed early – without any supper.

But Jake didn't mind. At least he knew he would never ever be asked to do the vacuuming again.

love from
Jake

SIMON JAMES

Simon James is an award-winning author and illustrator of books for children – creator of the much-loved character Baby Brains and of touching tales exploring a child's unique relationship with Nature.

ISBN 978-1-84428-522-8

ISBN 978–1-4063-0847-1

ISBN 978-1-4063-0846-4

ISBN 978-1-4063-0848-8

ISBN 978-1-4063-0202-8

ISBN 978–1-4063-0845-7

ISBN 978-1-4063-0849-5

ISBN 978-1-84428-467-2

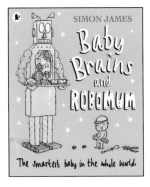

ISBN 978-1-4063-1338-3

"Drawing always opens up a very private and delightful world. It's easy to forget that drawing in itself is a kind of magic. Drawing is good for you!" SIMON JAMES

Available from all good bookstores
www.walkerbooks.co.uk